I Don't Know Why...
I Guess I'm Shy

Published by
Magination Press
An Educational Publishing Foundation Book
American Psychological Association
750 First Street, NE
Washington, DC 20002

For more information about our books, including a complete catalog, please write to us, call 1-800-374-2721, or visit our website at www.maginationpress.com.

Editor: Darcie Conner Johnston
Art Director: Susan K. White
The text type is Bookman
Printed by Phoenix Color, Rockaway, New Jersey

Library of Congress Cataloging-in-Publication Data

Cain, Barbara.
I don't know why...I guess I'm shy / written by Barbara Cain ;
illustrated by J.J. Smith-Moore
p.   cm.
Summary: Having been worried about bothering his neighbors
by talking to them, a shy boy searches the neighborhood for his lost dog
and finds the courage to speak.
ISBN 1-55798-596-0
[1. Bashfulness Fiction. 2. Dogs Fiction. 3. Lost and found possessions
Fiction. 4. Neighbors Fiction.] I. Smith-Moore, J.J., ill. II. Title.
PZ7.C1194Iaam 1999
[E]-dc21
99-20916
CIP

Manufactured in the United States of America
10 9 8 7 6 5 4 3 2 1

I Don't Know Why... I Guess I'm Shy

WRITTEN BY Barbara Cain

ILLUSTRATED BY J.J. Smith-Moore

MAGINATION PRESS • WASHINGTON, DC

Especially for you, Ahboo—BSC

To my nephew, Spencer Scott Smith—JJSM

Sammy Samson loved many things. He loved
tree forts and running shoes and butterflies and
boats. But most of all, he loved Sparky, his black
and white dog with black and white socks.

Sammy and Sparky were special friends. They ran together and they swam together. They biked together and they hiked together. You might even say they were forever together.

One spring day when the world was green and tulips looked like lollipops, Mrs. Samson said, "What a fine day for an afternoon stroll. Sammy, let's go down to the ice cream store."

"Can I bring Sparky?" Sammy asked.

"Of course you can," Mrs. Samson smiled. "Now where would we ever go without Sparky in tow?"

With one rattle of the leash, Sparky was at the door, and they were off to the ice cream store.

Along the way they passed Mrs. Pennington painting her fence.

Mrs. Pennington said "hi" to Mrs. Samson, who greeted her warmly.
She said "hi" to Sparky, who waved with his tail.
She said "hi" to Sammy, who said…nothing.

"Why don't you say hello to Mrs. Pennington?"
Sammy's mother whispered.

Sammy said quietly, "I don't know why…I guess I'm shy."

Next they met Mr. Miller building a birdhouse.

"Hi there, Samsons," Mr. Miller hailed. "What a big boy you've become, Sammy. How old are you now, young man?"

Sammy looked at the ground and studied his shoes. Mrs. Samson tugged at his sleeve. But Sammy continued to study his shoes.

"I wish I didn't have to talk," he thought, "I can't think of anything to say."

"Sammy just got a new pair of running shoes," Mrs. Samson explained. "And I guess that's what's on his mind today."

"Oh, that's all right," Mr. Miller said. "When I was a boy, and I once was a boy, you know, I used to think a new pair of sneakers was nearly as good as a trip to the moon."

9

As they crossed the court, Mrs. Samson said, "Mr. Miller is such a kind man. Why wouldn't you talk to him, or at least answer his questions?"

Sammy said, "I don't know why...I guess I'm shy."

"Hmmm," said Mrs. Samson. "Remember when you were a little tyke, and you and Mr. Miller used to watch birds together? He taught you some of their names and songs, and you loved chirping and chattering with him. What's different now? Why don't you want to talk to Mr. Miller anymore?"

"I still do want to talk to Mr. Miller," said Sammy. "But every time I start, the words get stuck!"

"What if you tried to un-stuck them?" Mrs. Samson chuckled.

"The wrong ones might come out," Sammy explained, "and then I would really sound double dumb!"

As they rounded the corner, they saw Mrs. Pinter planting peppers in her garden patch.

"What a lovely vegetable garden you have," Mrs. Samson said.

Sparky seemed to think so, too. He scampered through the garden and trounced on a turnip.

"You do have a frisky dog," Mrs. Pinter laughed. "Sammy, dear, what's your dog's name?"

Mrs. Pinter waited for an answer.
Mrs. Samson waited for an answer.
Even Sammy waited for an answer.

But an answer never came.

"Did you forget Sparky's name?" Mrs. Samson teased as they left the Pinters' house.

"I'd never forget Sparky's name is Sparky," Sammy insisted.

"Then why didn't you tell Mrs. Pinter his name?" Mrs. Samson gently asked.

"I don't know why...I guess I'm shy," said Sammy, but secretly he worried, "Maybe Mrs. Pinter is mad at Sparky for being so frisky."

Sammy stopped to hug Sparky and noticed a turnip leaf in one black and white paw. "But Sparky, YOU'RE not shy, are you?" he said.

"He sure isn't," Mrs. Samson agreed. "I wonder why he's not."

Sammy thought for a moment. "Well, maybe he's not scared of making Mrs. Pinter mad," he said.

Mrs. Samson nodded, "And I'll bet Sparky knows that even if she was a tad mad, she wouldn't stay that way for long."

Sammy grinned. "And Sparky doesn't have to talk to everybody like I do. Nobody tugs at his paw and says, 'Speak, Sparky, speak!'"

When they reached the ice cream store, Sammy hitched Sparky to a nearby tree.

"Wait right here, Sparky," he said, "and I'll be back in a jiffy."

Inside he gazed at a rainbow of flavors like deep purple boysenberry, pale green mint, and bright orange tangerine.

"And what would you like today, young man?" Mr. Daniels asked Sammy.

Sammy pointed silently to his favorite flavor.

When Mr. Daniels handed him a double dip chocolate chip, Sammy wanted to say thank you...but he didn't.

Do you know why?
Because Sammy felt shy.

Then Sammy looked at Mr. Daniels' good-humor face and thought, "I *can* do this. I *can* un-stuck these words. I *know* I can!"

"THANKS," he squeaked...but no one could hear.

"Say it again, and louder," Sammy told his voice, as he stood as tall as he could.

"THANK YOU! THANK YOU, MR. DANIELS!"

"Oh my," Mr. Daniels smiled broadly. "Such a nice young man deserves an extra treat," he announced, and he scattered a spoonful of sprinkles across Sammy's chocolate chip.

"Wow! Thanks a lot!" Sammy beamed, and marched out the door of the ice cream store.

Sammy and Mrs. Samson went to unhitch Sparky. But when they got to the tree, Sammy's stomach did cartwheels and he gulped very hard.

"Sparky's gone!" he shouted. "I can't find Sparky!"

Sammy grabbed the empty leash and ran as fast as his new shoes could carry him.

17

He ran past the Pinters' house.

"She won't be mad, she won't be mad," he muttered to himself when he saw Mrs. Pinter watering her new peppers.

"Did you see Sparky?" he called to her.

"Who?" she asked.

"Sparky, my dog, Sparky!"

"Oh, is that his name?" Mrs. Pinter asked with a twinkle. "Come to think of it," she said, "I did see him tearing up the hill toward the Millers' house."

18

Sammy flew up the hill and asked
Mr. Miller if he had seen Sparky.
"As a matter of fact I did,"
Mr. Miller said. "I saw him
darting across the court toward
the Penningtons' house."

Sammy darted too.

"Did you see Sparky?" he called to Mrs. Pennington.

"Indeed I did," Mrs. Pennington said. "I saw him whizzing up the street, heading toward the park."

"Sparky, I'll never find you unless I ask these people where you are,"
Sammy told himself as he ran through the park gate.

He asked a woman with a stroller if she had seen Sparky.
He asked a man with a cane if he had seen Sparky.
He asked a jogger with a frown if he had seen Sparky.

Everyone said, "Yes, there's a black and white pooch playing by the pond."

Sammy scurried to the pond.
But no Sparky was there.
Sammy flopped on the bench
and held his head in his hands.

"Oh, Sparky, where are you?"
he cried aloud.

"Where else can I go to find you?"
Sammy wondered as he shook
the empty leash.

"Did you chase a bird up a tree?
Or a rabbit through a tunnel?"

Sammy and Sparky rolled and
tumbled and squealed and yelped like two
playful puppies wrestling in the grass. Suddenly Sammy
looked up and saw a group of smiling faces and waving hands.

"Look, Sparky," he said. "There are all the people who
helped me find you."

"There's Mrs. Pinter, who sent me to the Millers'."
"There's Mr. Miller, who sent me to the Penningtons'."
"And there's Mrs. Pennington, who sent me to the park...
where I found YOU."

"It looks like Mrs. Pinter isn't mad at me.
And she isn't even mad at you, Sparky.
And I don't think Mr. Miller thinks I'm double dumb.
And everyone else was really nice to me."
Sammy said to Mrs. Samson,
"Maybe I worry too much
about getting in trouble."

"You know something, Sparky?"
said Sammy on the way home.
"I like our new friends all
waving goodbye.

And I think I know why
I used to be shy!"

29

What Is Shyness?

Shyness is a familiar cluster of feelings that can include fear, shame, embarrassment, and a painful self-consciousness in the presence of others. It is experienced to some degree by almost all children as they navigate the twists and turns of growing up. Shy children are generally aware of the same effective social skills as their more outgoing peers but have difficulty using them. They can be reluctant to talk to adults, wary of people they don't know, or uncomfortable in situations they haven't faced before. Most of all, they may be loath to draw attention to themselves, to occupy center stage, or to appear in "full view."

As a result, shy children often avoid participating in class discussions, even though they may be dedicated students. When they do force themselves to speak up, they may hardly talk above a whisper, or they may use the fewest number of words possible or speak in a monotone, hinting nothing of their emotions and revealing little about themselves. They may avoid performances such as a role in the school play, and resist invitations to parties or sleepovers. And although shy children may enjoy the exclusive company of individual friends, they may shrink from group activities and cleave to the margins, reluctant to presume a place of their own.

While research suggests a modest genetic link to shyness, studies also show that shyness can be greatly influenced by thoughtful interventions. Although shy children may continue to approach adults, large groups, and new situations warily, parents and others can most certainly help ease their concerns, unpleasant imaginings, and fears about failing, looking foolish, being criticized, or shunted aside.

How to Use This Book

This simple story line is intended to provide a working model for change in a young child attempting to overcome shyness. As Sammy considers reasons for his apparent reticence, gives himself encouraging pep talks, and tentatively tests the waters for a different outcome, he not only enjoys a prideful sense of accomplishment but also discovers that his fears of scorn and criticism are, after all, only imaginary. And ultimately, through his urgent desire to find his missing dog, he learns that most grown-ups are friendly and eager to offer a helping hand when given the chance. This story has been crafted to inspire the young reader to search similarly for techniques that can help him overcome shyness or any other interfering feelings.

The story is intended to stimulate open discussion between child and parent (or another trusted adult). By asking your child questions regarding Sammy's reluctance to talk to adults, you can help him or her locate the source of his or her own puzzling discomfort. You might ask,
- "Do you have any ideas about why Sammy didn't want to talk to Mr. Miller, who used to be his friend?"
- "What might have helped Sammy begin to talk?"
- "Sammy seemed a bit worried about making people mad or making a mistake. Do you have any ideas about where he got those ideas? Do you think most kids feel that way sometimes?"
- "What do you think Sammy will do the next time he sees one of his neighbors?"

Although this book focuses exclusively on shyness with adults, the underlying psychology (fear of anger, criticism, failure, and embarrassment) operates in other situations that trigger shyness—with peers, large groups, performances, and unfamiliar people and places. This story focuses on shyness with adults because children typically view this manifestation as less shameful than, say, shyness around peers, and they can therefore claim it more readily and discuss it more candidly.

In addition, guidelines for parents' behavior are offered throughout the story. Mrs. Samson poses thoughtful questions but doesn't probe or insist on answers. She reassures, makes gentle suggestions, and encourages self-exploration but does so with humor, affection, and unobtrusive interest.

How Parents Can Make a Difference

1

Provide easy access to other children by choosing, when feasible, to live in neighborhoods densely populated with children. Expose children to many adults and peers from as early an age as possible.

2

Make a habit of visiting nearby parks and playgrounds, which offer countless opportunities for spontaneous relating to other children and their parents. Bring familiar toys that invite interaction with children and conversation with adults. Try to allow play and chatter to evolve naturally, but if it doesn't, you can help your child by engaging her in an activity that is likely to draw the interest of other children, such as playing with a ball or another toy. When another child approaches, make it easy for the newcomer to join in as naturally as possible, and gently facilitate interaction between the children to get them started—then let your child manage on her own.

3

Become your child's booking agent. Arrange visits with playmates he has enjoyed in the past, meeting both at home and in other familiar settings. As your child grows more comfortable with certain people and places, start easing him into less familiar settings. You can do this, for example, by talking about a new place beforehand, by showing your child pictures if possible, or by taking along a known playmate. Afterward, gently reinforce your child's progress and positive outlook with comments such as, "Which animals did you like best at the zoo?" and "You looked like you were having so much fun on the water slide that I wanted to slide down it, too!"

4

Expose your child to your adult friends who relate comfortably with children. Include her in conversations with adult visitors, shop keepers, and familiar neighbors. Relay messages from adult acquaintances intended for the child; for example, tell her Mr. Jones asked how the Little League team is faring this year. If your child won't talk, perhaps she can start with a wave or other nonverbal form of communication like a "thumb's-up" gesture or a picture she drew, taking the focus off the verbal interaction.

5

Help your child "get out of himself" and think about another person rather than focus on his own discomfort. For example, if you and your child are walking your family dog and meet a neighbor, as Sammy does in this story, you might say to your child, "I'll bet Mrs. Rose is really happy that we walked by today and said hello. She hasn't been feeling well lately. I know just seeing you and Sparky will cheer her up. Kids and dogs really make grown-ups smile!"

6

Pets of all varieties are especially effective vehicles for helping shy children. Like Sammy in this story, a child's delight in and concern for her puppy or kitten can take the focus off herself, allowing for more spontaneous interaction. On walks through the neighborhood or visits to the park, her pet can spark an easy exchange with other children and adults, who may want to tell your child about their own pets—their names and antics and special traits. An un-self-conscious prattle will often follow.

7

Enroll your child in group activities. Choose those that match his special abilities and natural inclinations in order to maximize success and minimize failure. If he is reluctant to participate on, say, a soccer team, tell him, "It's okay to sit on the sidelines and watch. That's a good way to get experienced with soccer. It's a good start. As the days go on, it will probably get easier to go out and play, too." In this way you let your child know that you believe he can master his discomfort. Also, it is important to help your child experience success as he ventures out. Work with other adults in charge (the coach, the teacher, etc.) to facilitate your child's entry into the activity and his success with it once he is involved. Finally, a shy child's comfort level usually increases the smaller the group. However, while it is good to start with small groups, your ultimate goal is to help your child feel increasingly comfortable in larger groups, too. Slowly over time, kids can be helped to make this progression using the suggestions outlined here.

.

8

Resist the temptation to coax your child into speaking up or getting involved. Other complications can arise from this well-intentioned effort. A contest of wills between prodding parent and reluctant child can further increase her wish to withdraw. In addition, urging her to be more outgoing can strengthen her hidden concern that she is bad, blameworthy, or somehow flawed.

9

Bear in mind that in most instances, shy youngsters will generally find their own brand of coping with their emotions and relationships. In time, they will confidently move on, in their own adaptive style, with your gentle support. Parents are usually experts on their own children and often have a good idea what might be inhibiting them in a given situation. Talk supportively and gently to your child to find out what might be getting in the way, keeping in mind that "why" questions often shut children down. For example, you might say, "Maybe you're worried that you won't draw well enough in the art class, but the teacher just wants everyone to have fun and enjoy art. There's no right or wrong way to draw."

10

If your child's unease seems more than a phase, if it intensifies, if it is interfering with his normal development, if his spheres of activity diminish, if his circles of friendship narrow, or if a more generalized discomfort becomes apparent, you should seek guidance from a mental health professional. It is best to err in the direction of obtaining help sooner rather than later, because shyness can be a crippling problem for children if it continues for a long time.